THE ADVENTURES OF

Seymour & Hau

We can't wait to visit
Ledgeview Elementary!

Melanie +

Tom

"Travel is fatal to prejudice, bigotry, and narrow-mindedness, and many of our people need it sorely on these accounts. Broad, wholesome, charitable views of men and things cannot be acquired by vegetating in one little corner of the earth all one's lifetime."

-Mark Twain

Melanie Morse & Thomas McDade

Illustrated by: John Soleas & Jon Westwood

A **HONEY PUNCH** BOOK

Honey + Punch LLC - info@honeyandpunch.com

ISBN 978-0-9981725-0-7

Published by: Honey + Punch LLC

First Edition

The Adventures of Seymour & Hau: Ireland © 2016

For my Mama -MM

For Mom & Dad -TM

Thank you!

Wow!! So many wonderful folks to thank!! For starters we want to thank Ireland. You're amazing. The instant friendship and hospitality that was shown to us across the whole country was supreme! A very special thanks to; Fred Malzard at Malzard's Pub in Stoneyford & his girl Róisín for letting us use her name, the folks at Lawcus Farm Guest House, owners Ann-Marie Gisanne & Mark Fisher and their brilliant staff Robin Ribbers, & Julianne Maher, All-Ireland Hurling Champ Seán Meally for his expert hurling info & his boy Ciarán for lending us his name, John Buggy for his hurling knowledge, and for taking us to Star Hurley. Thanks to; Star Hurley for welcoming us into their shop, the young hurlers that gave us tips about hurling; Jamie Young, Jack Buggy, Harry Walsh, Shane Staunton, and Chris Korff. John Higgins of Galway who pulled a hurley out of his trunk and sent us home with it! Thank you to Caoimhin Mac Giolla Mhin, Padraic Walsh, Seán Mistéal and Vic Sinnott for your knowledge of Irish, and to Rianne Brouwer for her friendly nature.

Thank you to our family and friends!! Special thanks to; Kathy Boyd for your awesome editing & mastery of commas & quotation marks. To Mom Patty(for all the kid watching), Mom & Dad McDade (for all the Honey watching and the Irish wit), Aunt B, Mo Hourihane, and anyone we missed!! To Jacob, Elliot and Charlie for the inspiration, motivation, & love. To Grandpa Honan for bestowing your wealth of Irish history & family history upon us, we sure do miss you!

Ireland

TABLE OF CONTENTS

INTRODUCTION

ME

Hi, I'm Seymour and I'm 11. I live with my mom and two younger brothers. I love drawing, football, and playing the ukulele. I used to be a normal kid until Hau showed up. I'm actually still normal, if you call normal going on wild adventures and getting my life threatened to help kids from all over the world.  Besides that, everything is the same, except that I'm hanging with a mega-galactic alien, and my closet smells gross.

Oh, BTW, I like to make lists. That's my thing.

HAU

lobraee rejer AF-un nr ere ratydu ep lru ct eae whr... srbar ere

Translation

My name is Hau. Take me to your leader earthling. LOL! My people think I needed to learn some "life lessons," so they sent me to earth. Seymour is helping me to get back home. So far, the life lessons I learned are: I love Earth people, Earth food and TV, especially The Voice, and Ellen DeGeneres and Dr. Phil, but don't tell anyone about that last one. I live in Seymour's closet, and everyone here thinks I smell gross.

MY MOM

My mom's name is Helen, and she is the coolest mom on the planet. She doesn't yell... too much. I can't tell her about Hau, but she is getting suspicious. I heard her talking to my grandma on the phone, and she said, "That boy is acting so strange lately. He's always telling stories about different countries. It's almost as if he travels in his sleep." Can you believe she said that? I'd better be more careful. She also said, "...and his closet smells awful, I can't figure out what it might be." Let's hope she doesn't!

HOW I MET HAU

I swear, I thought this was SPAM until Hau stumbled out of my closet.

Incidentally, Hau loves SPAM, the food kind, not the email kind.

Hau's arrival - Inbox

To: Seymour
From: Morgeeta Dispatcher
Subject: Hau's Arrival

Seymour,

You have been chosen to help Hau regain his place on our planet. He has been sent to Earth to earn his way back. You will be sent on great adventures, face danger and help kids around the world. We cannot guarantee your safety but, you will be rewarded when your mission is complete. You will be tested and return tired but, no time will pass at home. We are watching and Hau's return home will depend on your success.

Best of luck,

Oruk
Dispatch Director
Morgeeta, Milky Way Galaxy

THE TELLUS

Hau has got this AWESOME little machine that he keeps in his pouch. It's called a TELLUS, and it "tells us" where we need to go and who we need to help. Get it? Tell Us. I'm dead serious, that's what it's called. It kind of looks like a cell phone with flashing lights all over it. It's connected to Hau's planet somehow. They know EVERYTHING that's happening on Earth. They are always watching us. Bizarre. There's a map on it, and a little black dot that blinks in the spot where we have to go. It also helps us with The Leap. There's a bunch of other buttons on it, too, but we haven't figure out what they do yet.

THE POUCH

OK, so Hau has this pouch. It's kind of like a kangaroo pouch but he can pull just about anything out of it—except maybe a baby kangaroo. They all have pouches on his planet. I have

no idea what's even in there. It's really random. I don't think even Hau knows, but I have seen him pull everything from a wheelbarrow to a "Kiss Me I'm Irish" t-shirt out of that thing. Now, if he could only pull out some soap....

THE LEAP CLOSET

It's really my bedroom closet. It looks like a normal bedroom closet: games on the shelf, clothes on the floor. The usual. However, when The Leap happens, the closet is totally NOT NORMAL. Once we shut the door, Hau pushes a button on the TELLUS, and everything turns the color of tie-dye. Then, it feels like you're on a crazy roller coaster ride and you land in a far away place. It is SO FUN! The Leap Closet is also Hau's bedroom... which is why it reeks.

IRELAND & HURLING

Here's a little information about Ireland and the super cool sport HURLING!

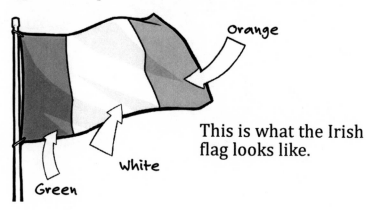

Orange

This is what the Irish flag looks like.

White

Green

This is what Irish words looks like.

Tá tú go hiontach!

That says "you are awesome" in Irish

FUN FACT

When you count in Irish, you use different words depending on if you're counting people or something else.

If there were 5 kids you'd say "cúigear páistí," but for 5 puppies it would be "cúig choileán".

Full name of Ireland: The Republic of Ireland

Location: Continent of Europe

The Official languages: Irish (Gaelic) & English

The money is called: Euros

Here are some other Irish phrases:

> **What is your name**? --- Cad is ainm duit?
>
> **Nice to meet you**. ---Is deas bualadh leat.
>
> **How are you?** --- Conas atá tú?

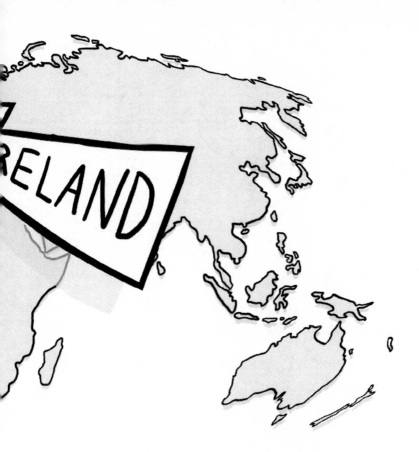

Hello --- Dia duit

Goodbye --- Slán

Can I stay up a little longer? --- An féidir liom fanacht i mo shuí beagán níos faide?

Thank you --- Go raibh maith agat

Yes --- Tá

No --- Níl

Friend --- Cara

Hurleys are made from the wood of an Ash tree

This is the Bas (pronounced BOSS)

Hurling is a rough and sometimes bloody sport that is amazing to watch.

- The stick you use is called a hurley or a hurl for short.

- The ball is called a sliotar. (You say it like SHH-LITH-AR)

- The field is called the "pitch", and it's 145 meters long and 90 meters wide. It's really big. Bigger than a football field!

- Each team has 15 players on the field at a time.

- Your uniform is called your "kit".

- The goalposts look like a big "H" with a net in the bottom. Like a soccer net mixed with American football goalposts.

- You get 1 point for hitting the sliotar through the top of the "H" and 3 points for hitting it in the net at the bottom of the "H", but you have to get it past the goalie, of course.

FINN MCCOOL

Finn McCool was a mythical giant, a hunter-warrior of Irish legend from many, many years ago. In Irish, his name is Fionn mac Cumhaill. The legend says that he's sleeping in a cave below Dublin, and he will wake up to defend Ireland when he's needed. COOL!

I COWABUNGA

"HAU! WE WON!!!"

I had just walked in from my soccer game, and my bedroom smelled like Hau, as usual. It's funny, but after soccer practice, Hau's "unique aroma" doesn't seem to hit me as hard. Could be that it blends in nicely with my shin guards and soccer socks.

Incidentally, when something smells really gross, my mom says it has a "unique aroma" 'cause it sounds nicer than "That really reeks!! PEEEEUUUUU!"

"HAU, DID YOU HEAR ME? WE WON!!" I shouted out again.

I flopped down on the bed. The game was SO AWESOME! My team, the Cosmos, won 4-3.

It was a close one, but my pal Charlie kicked it in the goal right at the last second. It was SO COOL! Everyone kind of freaked out and we rode him around on our shoulders for a while until his mom said, "Put him down right this second before you drop him on his head." Too bad Hau wasn't there. He would have been SUPER excited.

As I thought about Hau, I realized that he was awfully quiet. Usually he would have been bouncing around my room, making a mess, asking for food, and saying something like, "PLEEESE can I go to the soccer game next time?"

Something weird was going on.

"Hau?" I peeked in the closet. No Hau.

"Hey, man? Where are you?" I peeked under my bed. No Hau.

I looked in my drawers where he likes to hide sometimes. No Hau.

All of a sudden... "COWABUNGA!!!!!" Hau comes flying down from the top of my bookshelf and lands SPLAT on my head.

"SEYMOUR! Did you like my moves? Were you surprised? Did you see me swing in like Indian Jones? Did you miss me? Do you want me to do it again? Do you have a box of juice for me to drink?

2

How about a fry of french, or maybe 20 of those?"

Wow. Now I know how my mom feels when she asks me if I want to play the game where I see how long I can be quiet. Does your mom ever do that? Actually, I like when Hau talks. He cracks me up.

"First of all, It's IndianA Jones. Second of all, yes, I like your moves," I tell him.

Hau says, "And how about THIRD of all, you have some food for me!"

I was just about to go and grab him a snack when I hear, "SEYMOUR JOSEPH!!!" Oh, boy. Here we go again. Do you remember what happens when your mom calls you by your first AND middle name?

"Coming!" I say to my mom.

I walked into the kitchen, and you won't even believe it.

The kitchen was covered in FLOUR and HONEY, and my mom was standing there with her hands on her hips. When your mom has her hands on her hips it usually means she's looking for some answers. Unfortunately, I can't give my mom real answers when it comes to Hau, so I smiled and said in my sweetest, most charming voice, "Science experiment?"

"Humph," she grunted.

Mom: 819. Sweet Voice: 0. I lose. Again. However, I swear I saw a tiny teeny grin on my mom's face.

Incidentally, a "tiny teeny grin" is what happens to your mouth when you think something is a little funny, but you're supposed to be serious.

She handed me a broom and a sponge. I'm pretty sure you know what it means when your mom hands you a broom and a sponge.

I walked back into my room after cleaning up

Hau's mess. He was about to get the "what for."

Just in case you don't know what a "what for" is, it's like when your mom says, "You're in big trouble!" And you say, "What for?" And she says, "What for? You know what for! I'll give you what for." And then you get a time out.

"So, why the honey and flour?" I asked Hau. "You owe me one, pal!"

"But, I was just trying to make mesmen bread like Taymir's mom did in Morocco. It didn't taste very malicious though," Hau said, bowing his head. But I could tell he was just pretending to be sorry.

"Oh, shame on me!" he said dramatically, and then tumbled himself into the closet. He is so bizarre.

I started to laugh, 'cause MAN that guy is funny, but then I quick got on my serious face so I could give him a lecture.

Incidentally, it's hard to get on a serious face after laughing.

I was just wishing that I knew Hau's middle name so I could lecture him properly, when I heard that familiar sound.

2 LEAPING + LANDING

BBUUUZZZZAAAAPPPPT! BBUUUZZZZAAAAPPPPT! BBUUUZZZZAAAAPPPPT!

It was the TELLUS, and it was going off again.

When the TELLUS goes off, it's time to go. Someone needs help, somewhere in the world, and it doesn't matter if you've just been running around playing some seriously good soccer for the past two hours. It's just the way it is.

What happens next, always happens next.

1. I watch Hau's eyes pop open really big (like flying saucers).

2. He bangs his head on the clothes rack and knocks down all the hangers.

3. He searches through his pouch and tosses out random things that are in his way. Usually old food.

4. He says, "HA AH." (Did I mention he says things backwards sometimes?)

5. He finds the TELLUS and shouts out where we are going.

For some reason this never gets old. It's SUPER FUNNY every time!

This time he shouted, "We are going to County Galway, baby!" and added in a little spin and some jazz hands.

Incidentally, "jazz hands" are when you wave your hands back and forth with palms facing out and then palms facing in a whole bunch of times really fast. It's weird, but it makes an impression. Try it!

I reached for my backpack. "Where's County Galway?" I asked.

Hau handed me the TELLUS, and I could see the little black dot blinking on an island in the Atlantic Ocean: Ireland. We were going to IRELAND! That is SO COOL! We hadn't been there yet.

I remember my first grade teacher, Mrs. Houston, talking about Ireland. She said that St. Patrick's Day was a national holiday in Ireland. She also said that it rains a lot there, and it's really super green, which makes sense if it rains a lot. I'd be lost in this job without my teachers.

Ireland is part of the continent of Europe. It's an island, and it's only a hop, skip and a jump away from England and Scotland.

Incidentally, a "hop, skip and a jump away" just means it's pretty close. Sometimes your grampa might say that to you if you're on a long walk with him and you're getting tired and starting to complain. It means you're really close to your destination.

Just for the record, you can't actually hop, skip or jump to England or Scotland from Ireland, but you can definitely take a boat or a plane. People have actually swum from Ireland to Scotland, but it takes FOREVER, and I bet it's really tiring.

I quick changed out of my soccer gear, grabbed my backpack, shoved in my raincoat and headed for the closet. Hau was pretty close behind, singing "When Irish eyes are smiling"... He sure does learn a lot from TV.

It was time for The Leap. Best ride EVER!

Here's what happens. We go in my closet and shut the door. Then, it feels like we're on a roller coaster in the dark. The closet disappears and turns the color of tie-dye, like my Uncle Matt's shirts. We always hear this loud rumble, which is just Hau's stomach and not really part of The Leap. Then, it feels like you shoot up a hill and drop down another. Your stomach falls down to your toes, and then you spin like you're inside of a stretched-out Slinky. Then you're up and down, you shoot to the right, and then left and then swing upside-down. It's all over in about 2.5 seconds. It is SO FUN!

I really hope you get to try it sometime!

Of course, you can't have a leap without a landing. This time I was pretty lucky. I landed with a smooshy wet plop. Pain scale = 5 out of 10.

I looked around. The sky was full of huge big fluffy white and gray clouds. We were on a tiny beach just at the edge of a huge body of water. The Atlantic Ocean. There were some fishing boats close by, but they were just sitting in the mud. Not floating at all. Must have been low tide. I learned about the tides in science class with Mr. Hurley. Sometimes my mom says my room smells like low tide.

The seashore was mostly rocky with some fluffy spongy grass around. There were some stone walls surrounding houses, and behind me I could see some smallish hills and pine trees. One thing's for sure... it was GREEN! The greenest green of all greens. I'm talking GREEN.

Turns out, we were in a very small town called Spiddal. It was on the west coast of Ireland in the county of Galway. Looked pretty AWESOME to me.

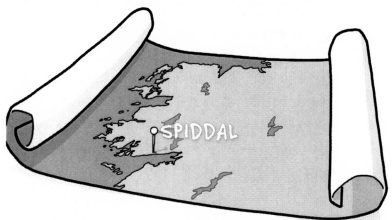

SPIDDAL

Now, where was Hau? I looked around the rocks near the shore and up and down the beach. Finally, I spotted him. He was floating on his back in the water with a seagull standing on his belly.

"Hey man, come on, lets go!" I called.

"I'm TRYING, but this guy is tickling me. HAHAHAHAHAHA!!!"

laughed Hau. He started to backstroke over to me, which is not easy when you are cracking up, even if you are a mega-galactic alien who can leap around the world and sort-of fly.

When Hau got to shore, the seagull flew away, and we did the bruise count contest like we always do after we take The Leap. I only had two bruises this time, and Hau had none since he landed in the water. He did get a mouthful of salt water, which he said he "enjoyed thoroughly," so I won. Lucky me. He did his sad dance, 'cause he likes to win, even if it's a bruise contest. His sad dance is as equally entertaining as his happy dance. It's really just a breakdance move called The Worm and then he stands up and pulls his pouch over his head.

Just then, I saw some movement out of the corner of my eye. I turned to see a boy. This must be the kid. It's always the first kid we see. This time it was two kids, actually. One boy and one girl. I technically saw the boy first so it must be him. The girl looked younger than the boy and was drawing a picture in the sand with a stick. He was sitting on a stone wall tossing a ball up and down and looking REALLY sad. It was pretty easy to tell that this was the guy who needed our help.

3 THE HURLEY

Hau went to go hide in one of the empty boats nearby and I walked up to the kid. He said "hi" to me like this: "Dia duit." I guessed it meant "Hello" in Irish. I was correct. His name was Ciarán. You say it like this: KEY-RON and he was super friendly but definitely super sad. His shoulders were slumpy, and I could tell he was trying to smile but it wasn't really working. The girl was his little sister, Róisín. You say it ROW-SHEEN. Ciarán and Róisín could speak both English AND Irish.

Ciarán had brownish hair that was a bit curly and he was about the same size as me. He had freckles. Róisín had kind of reddish hair, and her face looked like Ciarán's, freckles and all.

I have to sidetrack us for a second. I actually didn't even know people spoke Irish, which is totally different than English! Did you? I thought they just spoke English with an Irish accent. Basically, everyone does speak English, but it turns out that lots of folks in Ireland speak Irish, too. Sometimes the language is called Irish Gaelic. In fact, the town of Spiddal has a whole school that teaches Irish and kids come there from all over Ireland just to learn the language. People are extra good at speaking Irish in Spiddal.

(Sidetrack means when you're talking about one thing, and then you think of something else, so you st art talking about that instead... like I just did. Now... on with the adventure!)

Suddenly, we heard a big splash, and I knew I had better tell them about Hau, and fast. See, here is what always happens. There is no way around it.

1. Hau hides. In this case he was hiding in a boat. BUT, he got curious and tried to get out when the boat got tippy, 'cause boats get tippy, and he plopped over the side. Hau is a great swimmer. It also helps that he can't sink. He only floats. Like a beachball.

2. I say, "Hi" and "Sorry" for whatever we broke. This time we didn't even break anything. Not yet, anyway.

3. I tell the kid I'm here to help.

4. The kid is totally confused because how the heck did I know to come and help?

5. I explain about Hau because:

   a.) If someone sees him too soon or they are not ready, they could run off, never to be seen again. Although that's never happened, it is a possibility.

   b.) It's not nice to surprise people with a watermelon-sized, flying, bizarrely shaped, eat-everything-in-sight mega-galactic alien. You need to give them some warning. It's only fair.

6. The kid totally gets it because kids totally get stuff that adults don't get.

7. The kid tells us the problem.

8. We get moving.

9. WAIT—first, we feed Hau. Then, we get moving.

As we walked toward the splash, we heard three more splashes. We spotted Hau trying to climb back into the boat but falling back into the water every time the boat tipped. We all looked at each other and started cracking up. Hau looked at us and started laughing, too.

Ciarán thought Hau was cool and Róisín LOVED Hau. She even hugged him and did not seem to mind the smell at all. She said it was a good thing he was green because he would blend into most everything around. She totally got it.

Ciarán told us what was wrong and why he was so sad. He said he had been playing in their backyard with his sister, pushing her on the swing, when he decided to practice a bit for his big hurling match. He went to go get his hurley, which he always kept in the front hall with his helmet, and his hurley was gone. Just vanished.

At that point I had to ask Ciarán to "back up." Sometimes, "back up" means actually move back—like in school when you see a frog on the playground and everyone crowds around it until the teacher says "back up, back up," and you raise your hand to try to be the one who gets to pick it up and release it back into the woods.

This time, "back up" meant: Please go back in your story because I have no idea what you are talking about. I had never heard of a hurley or hurling, so how could I help until I knew what we were looking for? The only "hurley" I've ever heard of is my science teacher, Mr. Hurley. WELL, it turns out that **hurling** is a SUPER AWESOME sport and that a **hurley** is the stick you use to play it.

Let me explain:

Hurling is a very old sport that dates back to something like 3000 years ago! It's kind of like a mixture of lacrosse, baseball, soccer, hockey, golf, rugby and even whack-a-mole, and maybe a few more things. Here's how you play:

1. You get a hurley. It's a stick that looks like this.

2. You get a ball. It's called a sliotar. You say it like SHH-LITH-AR, and it looks like a baseball but with a little snakey material sticking out.

3. You get on your local team. In Ireland, you play on the team in the town or neighborhood where you live. That's the way it works. There's no playing for a different town. That's frowned upon.

4. The field is called a "pitch," and it looks like a mix between a soccer field and an American football field, only bigger. There is a goal on each end of the field that looks like huge "H", with a soccer net attached to the bottom of the "H".

5. You run up and down the field with your hurley, and you can bounce the sliotar on your stick, hold it in your hand for 4 steps, whack it with your hurley to your teammate (like a baseball), or golf it off the ground.

6. If you hit the sliotar into the net it's called a GOAL, and you get 3 points for your team. If you hit it over the goal posts its called a POINT, and it's worth 1 point for your team.

Got all that? I was really confused at first, but now I get it and it's SO FUN!!! I'm not kidding, you HAVE to try it.

So, Ciarán was missing his hurley, and the worst part was that his big championship game was TODAY!

"Why don't you just get a different hurley?" I asked him. Seemed like a simple fix. We always look for the simple fix first. Sometimes that works. When I played baseball the coach just brought a whole bunch a bats and we all used them.

Hau was eager to help, too. He started pulling things out of his pouch. "How 'bout this, or this or this... ?" he sang, as he pulled out a broom, a hockey stick, a baseball bat, a snow scraper, a lacrosse stick, a ping pong paddle, a coffee table book of different toilets around the world, a teapot (with mint tea that was still hot—how does he do that??), and a hamburger.

Hau ate the hamburger. "I meant, except for that!"

Ciarán stared at him like he was bizarre. First-time pouch see-er. Happens to everyone. After his **pouch-shock***, he was able to answer.

*Pouch-shock: when someone sees Hau pull random stuff out of his pouch for the first-time, and they can't understand how those things fit in there, and I can't explain it 'cause neither do I.

23

Ciarán explained why we couldn't do the simple fix.

"For starters, we have no hurley stores around here. AND you don't just use any old hurley, you have to use the right size. It's got my special wrap on the handle. I scored a lot of goals and points with it. It's got a tooth mark from my dog on the bas (the big flat end of the hurley). Plus, my grandfather gave it to me. He was a champion All-Ireland hurler from Kilkenny when he was young. So, there are a lot of reasons. My little sister plays, too, and she said I could use hers, but it's too small for me. I need the one I've been practicing with all season. It's the BIG MATCH. You just have to use your own."

> Incidentally, an "All-Ireland hurler" means you won the biggest hurling game (or match, as they say in Ireland) of the year. And it means you're AWESOME at hurling.

Sounded perfectly reasonable to me. It was the big game. You need your hurley. That's that. Now we needed to find it.

"OK, so first things first, are you SURE it was in your front hall?" I asked him.

"I always keep my hurley with my helmet. I slide the hurley right through my helmet so it's easier to carry. And then I keep them stuck together."

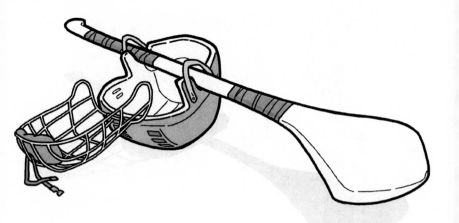

"Gotcha. Let's go back to your front hall and retrace your steps to see if we can find any clues," I said.

Incidentally, my mom told me about retracing your steps. What you do is go back to the place where you last knew you had something and do everything over again from that spot. She told me that it doesn't include accidentally re-breaking a window when you lose your baseball. She probably should have told me that sooner. But that's another story.

4 RECTANGLE FINGER

Ciarán took us back to his house to show us where he last saw his hurley. He told us a little more about the sport of hurling on the way.

Hurling is REALLY popular in Ireland. There are 32 counties in Ireland. Kind of like how the United States has 50 states. Most of the counties have their own hurling team that will represent

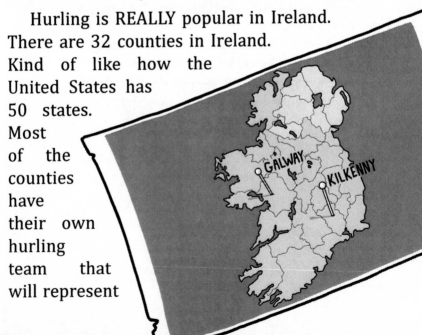

GALWAY

KILKENNY

their county in the All-Ireland matches. You ALWAYS root for your own county. Like when you "root, root, root for the home team." Ciarán roots for Galway, which is the county he is from, but his mom roots for Kilkenny 'cause that's where she is from. The All-Ireland final match is a HUGE game, as big as the mega-large giant championship football game in the USA.

Incidentally, Ciarán, has a SUPER cool accent when he speaks English, and he calls me "mate" a lot, which means "friend" or "pal" in Ireland.

We arrived at his front hall. His helmet was still there, but he was right, no hurley.

He retraced his steps:

1. He was practicing soloing* in the front yard.

2. Róisín asked him to push her on the swings.

*Soloing: is when you toss the ball onto the flat part of your hurley and balance it there while you run at top speed toward the goal while guys are chasing you and trying to knock the ball off your stick. It is SO HARD... but FUN!!

3. He took off his helmet, put the hurley through it and set it in the front hall against the wall.

4. He went outside to push Róisín for about 20 minutes, and when he came back in to get his hurley, it was gone.

5. He and Róisín searched the house and walked down to the beach to see if their dog had dragged it over there, when they remembered that their Dad had brought the dog to work that day, so it couldn't have been Noogy.

6. They were sitting at the beach when Hau and I arrived, and you know the rest.

We searched the entire house again and even checked to see if it was behind the refrigerator or something random like that. Nothing! It was gone!

Hau was stumped, too, but, he never gives up. He pulled a magnifying glass out of his pouch and started searching the rooms with a fine-tooth comb.

Note: You don't actually use a fine-tooth comb for this, it just means you look super awesomely good and careful.

Hau kept saying, "Nothin' here, mate. Nothin' here, mate!"

As Hau looked at every inch of the room, I noticed that the window was open a crack, and I could see some dirty fingerprints on the glass.

The fingerprints were weird because they looked like 9 normal fingerprints and one big smushy fingerprint with a little rectangle on the right hand where the pointer finger would be. They looked like this:

I never saw fingerprints that looked like that before.

"Hey Hau, hand me that magnifying glass!"

We all took a look at the fingerprints.

"Oooooh, rectangle-finger," said Hau, nodding very professionally. Hau is SO FUNNY.

The fingerprints were on the outside of the glass.

"Is this window usually open, Ciarán?" I asked.

"Not usually. It faces the wind and so my mum keeps it closed because it blows all of my sister's drawings off the fridge when it's open. Plus, it's a bit chilly today, and she would never open it while we have the heat on."

Incidentally, my mom is the same way, she's always yelling, "SHUT THE DOOR! YOU'RE LETTING THE HEAT OUT!"

We went outside to take a closer look.

Meanwhile, we saw Hau through the window. He had stayed inside to look for clues. He was doing his happy dance and pointing and jumping up and down. He's very excitable.

"Clue, clue, cluuuue, clue, clue, cluuuue, clue, clue, clue, clue cluuuuuuuuuuuuue!" sang Hau to the tune of jingle bells.

He was pointing to what kind of looked like a prickly, dotted footprint, but I wasn't sure. It wasn't your normal average footprint. We rushed back inside to check it out.

"That sure does look like a hurling boot, if ye ask me!" said Ciarán. "Good clue, Hau mate!"

Hau was thrilled at being called "mate." He flew in the air a little, from thrilledness.

Incidentally, I would call them cleats, but in Ireland they call them boots.

Boots = cleats

Not winter boots, not hiking boots—cleats like soccer cleats. Get it? Also, they call their hurling uniform a kit, in case you were wondering.

Kit = uniform

We looked closer and noticed that the boot-print was sandy. Another important clue.

30

Just then, Róisín walked in and said, "Mum will be mad at you wearing your hurling boots in the house again!"

"I never did, see there, mine are outside and never came in. Last time I had to vacuum the

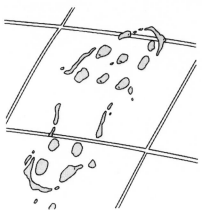

whole house for wearin' 'em in. Never doin' that again!" Ciarán said.

I get that. I think we all get that.

Just **for good measure***, I checked to see if Ciarán's hurley boots were the same size as the boot-prints. Nope. The prints were bigger. Bigger prints = bigger feet.

> *For good measure: means to double make sure something is correct. Also, it can mean to add a few extra, just in case. For example: I added a few more cans of soda pop to the picnic basket, for good measure.

So, what do we have here:

1. An open window that is usually closed.
2. A weird rectangle fingerprint on the outside of the window.
3. Sandy hurling boot-prints near where the hurley was, that do not match Ciarán's feet.
4. A missing hurley.

31

At this point I smelled a MAJOR rat.

"Dude, someone took your hurley, and by the look of these clues, it was another hurler. What time is the game?"

5 A FULL IRISH

We had exactly 4 hours and 3 minutes to find the missing hurley and get Ciarán to his championship game.

We decided to start back at the beach, since because of the sandy boot-prints, and maybe we could find a clue from there. Róisín stayed home just in case the hurley showed up. Before we could leave there was just one thing left to do. Can you guess?

Feed Hau. He is useless without food.

Róisín was all over it. She had whipped up what she called a Full Irish Breakfast in no time flat.

A Full Irish Breakfast is this:

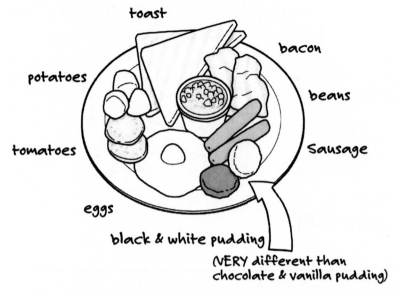

toast

bacon

potatoes

beans

tomatoes

Sausage

eggs

black & white pudding

(VERY different than chocolate & vanilla pudding)

It was A LOT of food. I honestly think even Hau was full... which does not happen very often. The Full Irish created a Full Hau! HAHA! He put his hands on Róisín's shoulders, looked at her very seriously, and said, "You are my favorite of all humans." Then he gave her a big hug and a slightly slimy kiss on the cheek.

My grandma always says, "The way to a person's heart is through their stomach." I believe this is also true for mega-galactic aliens.

Róisín giggled, hugged him back, and off we went, with Hau happier than I had ever seen him. He even got in the backpack voluntarily! I think he was too full to walk.

We walked over to the beach. As we walked, Ciarán started asking me all sorts of questions. Mostly he wanted to talk about American football. Turns out, the kids in his town LOVE American football. He knew all about the mega-large giant championship football game in the USA and even had a favorite team.

Incidentally, his favorite team was not my favorite team, but if I know anything, it's that you don't argue sports with a new friend.

How COOL that he knew about American football. And how was it that I had never even heard of hurling? Well, at least not until now!

We continued talking about American football, Gaelic football, soccer, hurling, candy, school, all sorts of things. His favorite candy is called a "Crunchie." It's a bar of chocolate and inside it's, well, crunchy. I got to try one while I was in Ireland. It reminded me of sponge candy, but Ciarán said he never heard of that. Have you ever heard of sponge candy? If not you need to go find some and eat some this instant. It's SO YUMMY!

Hau, of course, had to chime in. He burst out of the backpack and exclaimed, "MY favorite candy is called an EVERYTHING BAR. It's when you take Snickers™, and Twix™, and Skittles™, and M&M's™, and gum, and Starburst™ and 3 Moosekateers, and you smush, smush, smush it all together into one BIG bar and eat it. MALICIOUS!!!!"

I'm going to let him keep "Mooskateers." It's too awesome to correct.

I also found out that Ciarán and I had A LOT in common, even though we live all the way across the ocean from each other. We both love climbing trees, playing video games, skateboarding, superhero movies and comics, and we both do NOT love, peas, the dentist, bedtime and cleaning the bathroom. How about you?

We were almost to the beach when we saw a few kids who were walking toward the hurling pitch with their hurleys. They waved us over.

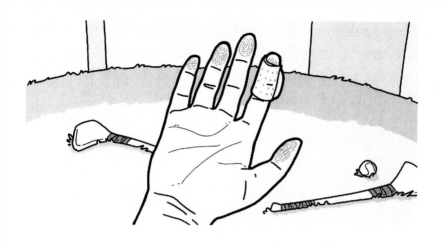

6 THE PLASTER

"Haigh, Ciarán, want to come practice with us?" they called.

Ciarán told me later that when you say "hi" to your pals in Irish, it sounds like "hi" but is spelled like "haigh." I said, "Wow, how do you like them apples?" Hau said, "Apples? Do we have apples? May I please have those apples?"

As we walked up to the kids, Ciarán whispered to me, "Let's not mention the missing hurley." He was the best player on the team and the **free taker,*** and he didn't want to worry his mates.

> **Free taker: is not only the best player on the hurling team but also the kid who gets to start with the ball when there is a foul. You DEFINITELY DON'T want your free taker to be missing their hurley.*

I grabbed Hau and stuck him back in my backpack, mostly because Hau can not keep a secret. He protested, but then I heard him say, "Thanks for the lift, brother."

The kids' names were Pádraic, Jack, Seán, and Killian. Ciarán told them that he couldn't practice with them just then because he was showing me around the town. He explained that I was in town visiting and didn't have much time, so we had to run off.

"Aw, too bad, mate!" said Pádraic. "See you in a bit. We are going to crush at the game tonight!"

"Yeah! See you then!" Ciarán smiled at his mates, but I could tell he was worried. We didn't have much time.

Just as we were rushing away Killian yelled, "Hey, you know what? We just saw Séamus!"

We slowed down.

"Who's Séamus?" I asked Ciarán.

Just so you know, you say it like SHAY-MUS.

"Oh, he's the best player for the other team. Really a brilliant hurler. He's the free taker on his team. He actually lives on Inishmaan, which is just out there in the water, it's one of the Aran Islands— the one in the middle. I wonder why he was here so early? The game isn't for 3 hours and 27 minutes."

Killian continued to call out to us: "It looks like he's got a bit of an injury. He cut his finger with a fishing hook. That's good news for us. He may not be as tough to play against today!"

I stopped cold. I wasn't actually cold. It just means you just stop, boom, exactly right where you are, all of a sudden.

I turned back to the kids. "Wait! Did you just say he injured his finger? Which finger?" I asked.

"He had a plaster on this right pointer finger." Killian said.

I found out pretty quickly that a "plaster" means a "band-aid" in Ireland.

"WAIT!! Where did you, uh, mates, see him?" I decide to try out the word. They looked at me like I was bizarre, but then Pádraic piped up.

"He was just heading to his boat. Seemed in a bit of a rush, too. In fact ye just missed him by about tree minutes. You can still see his boat just there, headin' home."

Tree = three with an Irish accent

"THAT'S IT!! The weird fingerprint!!" I shouted.

"THAT'S IT!!" exclaimed Ciarán. Eyes like flying saucers.

"DAT'S IT!!" yelled Hau from inside the backpack.

Pádraic, Jack, Seán and Killian stared at us.

"Heh, heh. I love fingerprints? Nice to meet ya,

gotta go, lots to do, little time, Adios, Ciao, Cheerio, fingerprint!!" I just yelled out random goodbye things. We had no time to explain. We ran toward the beach.

The kids all looked a little confused but continued on their way to the pitch.

We bolted to the edge of the water. We could see Séamus speeding away in his boat. He wasn't even halfway home yet.

"We need a boat! Let's go get him!!" Ciarán was so MAD.

7 THE PROOF

"Hang on, we need to be smart right now. We can't be POSITIVE he has it and we don't have time to go on a wild goose chase," I said, as I let Hau out of the backpack.

> Incidentally, a "wild goose chase" is when you run around looking for something that you probably won't ever find 'cause it probably isn't there.

"Well, that kid is always doin' somethin' malicious, and I don't mean the delicious malicious." Ciarán winked at Hau who was twirling around with a long piece of tape or something.

Malicious actually means: characterized by malice; intending or intended to do harm.

Delicious actually means: highly pleasing to the senses, especially to taste or smell.

To Hau, malicious means delicious. Totally different things but they rhyme, and English is not Hau's first language, or even second, I think. He does his best.

"What's that you have, Hau?" asked Ciarán.

"Oh dis?" He held up the tape thing.

"Dis is my new pretend snake I just found. It does not even bite at all. Seymour is afraid of snakes. If he sees one he screams like a tiny little cute baby. But, this one will not make him scream like a tiny little baby. Right, Sey?"

Oh, boy. Told you he can't keep a secret.

"Hey! That is actually tape from a hurley stick! And it be the same color I had on mine! Green! For good luck! It was starting to fall off from where my dog chewed it! I was going to mend it before the big game today!" shouted Ciarán.

I inspected the hurley tape. Sure enough, chew marks! It had to be Ciarán's!

"Where did you get this Hau?"

"I found it right there!" Hau stuck out his long

green finger and pointed right to where Séamus's boat would have been. The imprint from the boat was still in the sand AND, there were hurley boot-prints in the sand.

"Ciarán, bring your foot here!" Ciarán knew exactly what I meant. He measured his foot next to the print and sure enough... the print was bigger!

"Rhinoculars?" said Hau casually, and he handed me a pair of binoculars. Every so often he has just the right thing in that pouch, even though he may not have the exact right word.

I peered through the binoculars. I could see the back of Séamus as he drove the fishing boat toward home. Ciarán told me that the kids on the Aran Islands usually have their own boats and learn to drive them really young so they can get back and forth to stuff on the mainland. I thought that was SO COOL. But I wasn't so sure Séamus was so cool. He seemed like he was so UNCOOL.

I handed the binoculars to Ciarán. He gasped.

"I see it!! That's my hurley! Look!! Right there sticking out of his bag!"

It was true. Séamus was wearing a backpack and you could see the bas end of the hurley, and you could even see the tape was coming off!

Rectangle fingerprint, hurley boot-print, Séamus's plaster on the right index finger, Ciarán's hurley tape.

I think we had enough proof. We had proof coming out of our ears.

Now, we just needed a boat.

8 SALTY DOG

Where were we going to get a boat?

Hau started digging around his pouch, but the best he could come up with was a tiny canoe he had swiped from my grampa's model train set. It has a lake that the trains go around, and there WAS a canoe in it, and yes... it's AWESOME.

"Uh, that's a bit small, mate, but nice try" laughed Ciarán. Hau looked proud of his nice try.

"Don't ye lads have anyting better to do than starin' at the water?" said a voice.

We all jumped, and Hau burrowed himself into the sand, like a groundhog. Somehow he hadn't been noticed. Phew.

The voice came from an old fisherman. A kinda grumpy old fisherman from what I could tell. He looked like a fisherman, too. He had wild white hair that seemed trapped under his black hat, a big thick sailor sweater and yellow rubber pants. He is what my grandpa would call a real "Salty Dog."

Incidentally, a "Salty Dog" is something you might call a sailor or a fisherman who's been out on the sea a lot, 'cause of the salt water.

"Um, sorry sir, we will be getting on our way," said Ciarán.

Ciarán whispered that Salty Dog is always in a bad mood and that we should stay out of his way. In the town of Spiddal, everyone knows everyone, so no one is a stranger. He said if we don't hurry up, Salty Dog will probably make us do some chores. That is how small Spiddal is. You can get a chore from anyone, not just your mom.

I quickly and sneaky-like plucked Hau out of the ground, like a beet, a big green beet, and squished him, you guessed it, into my backpack.

We needed a boat, and fast. Or a plane. That would be faster. Maybe a helicopter. Heck, I would ride on the back of a whale if it were available right now.

Actually, I would ride on the back of a whale any old time. Whales are SO AMAZING! I was just adding "ride a whale" to my mental list of things to do, when Salty Dog barked at us again.

"Hey, you two! Come over here and help me wit me fishing gear," he called.

My mom told me that I always need to respect my elders. She said if your elder asks you to do a chore, you help and no groaning.

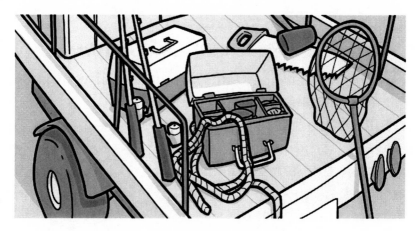

Incidentally, you should never help strangers unless your adult is with you. That is just a bad idea. Never ever do it without your adult. Got it? Give me a thumbs up.

Unfortunately, Salty Dog was not a stranger to Ciarán. He was his Dad's good friend, and apparently, he was told to respect his elders, too.

"Let's just help quick and get moving," whispered Ciarán to me.

We both hurried over to the truck and began to load the fishing poles, tackle boxes and bait buckets onto Salty Dog's boat.

We didn't have time for this. We had a hurley to find and a championship hurling match to get to!!!

Suddenly, Hau yelled out of the backpack, "Hurley, hurley, hurley stick!!"

"Hau, SHHHH!" I shushed toward the backpack.

"What did ye say?" Salty Dog looked at me.

49

"Um, hurley stick?" said me.

"What of a hurley stick?" asked Salty Dog

Ciarán could not stand it anymore. If we didn't get that stick back soon it would be too late. We were down to 2 hours and 58 minutes till game time, and who knows how long he would keep us doing chores.

"That kid stole my hurley, and if we don't get it back soon, I'm going to miss the championship hurling match today!" Ciarán blurted out, pointing at Séamus's boat way way off in the distance.

"What?!? What are ye talking about?" asked Salty Dog.

"He's taking my hurley over to Inishmaan, so I'll miss the game!"

Salty Dog got a very strange look on his face. At first he looked kind of bizarre. Then, he actually smiled and said, "Well, if it's one thing I know, you never take another man's hurley. Why didn't ye say so? Get in the boat boys, we are going full speed ahead!"

That sounded good to me! We had a ride!! It wasn't a whale, but it would do. We hopped in the boat and took off like a rocket.

I peeked in the backpack. "Sorry I shushed you pal. You got us a ride—good work!" I told Hau.

"No problemo, mate," smiled Hau. I helped him climb out of the backpack and hide on top of the standing shelter of the boat, so he could have a good view as we raced toward Inishmaan and Séamus.

Salty Dog said he could get us there fast and to hold on tight.

So, we did.

Full speed ahead, indeed!

9 TWO FOR JOY

We bounced and bumped over the waves as the boat headed toward the island of Inishmaan. Turns out, after the grumpy wore off, Salty Dog was a real talker. Here is what he told me about the Aran Islands on the boat ride. It's been a while, and so, it's time for my favorite thing... a list.

1. There are 3 Aran Islands. Inishmaan is the one in the middle.

2. Only about 160 people live on Inishmaan, so, everyone knows everyone there. That should make it pretty easy to find out where Séamus lives!

3. The other two islands are called Inishmore and Inisheer.

4. Inishmore is the biggest of the three. (or tree as they say in Ireland)

5. Inisheer is the smallest one, but even though

it's the smallest, it has more people than Inishmaan.

6. Inish means "island". In case you haven't figured that out yet.

7. There are lots of COOL rock walls and forts and stone structures on the islands and no one really knows exactly who built them or why they got built. Isn't that BIZARRE?

8. The islands are about 15 miles across the ocean from Spiddal.

We continued to bounce and get lots of spray from the ocean in our faces. I pulled on my raincoat,

super glad I remembered to bring that from home, and peeked up on top of the standing shelter to check on Hau.

He was holding on to a flag pole looking greener than usual. "Seymour, I'm seasick!" Then he laughed. "But not Sey sick. Get it? AHAHAHAHA!"

Hau cracks me up.

Salty Dog wasn't affected by the waves and bouncing. He had his sea legs, as my Grampa would say.

Incidentally, having "sea legs" means that you don't feel all wobbly and seasick when you are on a moving boat. You just feel normal, like you've on a regular floor on dry land.

He was focused on speeding the boat through the water. I could tell we were getting pretty close to shore, even though the ocean was spraying tons of salt water in my face. I decided I'd better stick Hau back in the backpack.

"Pssstt, Hau, hop in." I opened the backpack and he jumped in. "You OK, pal?" I asked him.

"I'm OK, pal. I could use a Full Irish," Hau smiled, hopefully.

"You just had one!" I laughed as I zipped him in. Hungry, hungry, Hau.

Suddenly, Salty Dog yelled out over the sound of the motor and the ocean.

He said, "Look over there, lads. See there?"

He pointed to some birds flying near the shore.
Then he began to recite a poem:

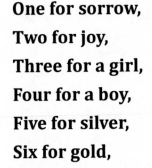

One for sorrow,

Two for joy,

Three for a girl,

Four for a boy,

Five for silver,

Six for gold,

**Seven for a secret never
to be told,**

Eight for a wish,

Nine for a kiss,

**Ten a surprise you must
not miss!**

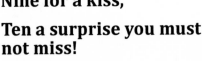
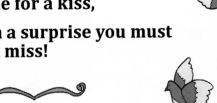

Ciarán told me it was a very old Irish nursery rhyme and a legend about magpies. I knew what a mud-pie was, but not a magpie. Turns out, a magpie is a bird, and some people believe that poem is true. Like, if you see one magpie you will have sorrow, two magpies you have joy, and so on. The numbers mean how many magpies you have to see for the thing to happen. Get it? Five magpies would be pretty AWESOME, but I hope I never see nine.

Sure enough, there were two birds flying and they were magpies. Two for joy. Sounds good to me. Let's hope the poem was right!

Salty Dog docked the boat and wished us good luck as we leapt onto shore. He said he couldn't stay to take us back because he had to get to one of the other islands for work. I noticed a shiny medal on a chain around his neck. It had bounced right out of his sweater with all of the bouncing from the waves.

"What's that medal?" I asked.

"Ah, don't ye be worrying about it." He tucked it back in quickly. "Now go find that hurley stick, and get to the game. I'll be hoping to be back in time to watch ye play, Ciarán."

And with that, Salty Dog sped back out into the Atlantic Ocean.

We waved goodbye and Ciarán did a quick time

check as I let Hau out of the backpack and shoved my raincoat in. Hau hugged the ground.

"Sweet land, I love you," he said.

"2 hours and 31 minutes until game time." Ciarán looked really worried.

I wasn't worried at all. Well, maybe a little worried. OK, actually a lot worried. Séamus

could be anywhere. The hurley could be anywhere!

"Don't worry Sey, we got this!" said Hau very positively.

I sure hoped he was right.

10 INISH MAN O' MAN

The island of Inishmaan was completely BIZARRE and totally AMAZING.

One thing that they have in Ireland is mist. I haven't mentioned the mist yet. It's not always misty, but when it is, it is the mist of all mists. When I was little I used to call it "tiny rain." It feels like a mini-shower on your face.

Inishmaan was especially misty that day. I looked around. It kind of looked like the moon but with tons and tons of rock walls, for no apparent reason. They didn't seem to keep anything in or anything out. Rock walls as far as the eye could see!

Ciarán told me that all those rock walls were made for a few different reasons. The main reason was to clear the rocks off the grass so people could farm. It's kind of hard to plant crops with tons of rocks in the way. The Aran islands are SUPER rocky. So, what do you do with a big pile of rocks to get them out of the way? You make a wall. When the wind and rain are really wild, you can also crouch down next to a rock wall and you won't get so wet. The walls also turned out to be good for marking property, but not so good for holding in sheep because they can jump right over them.

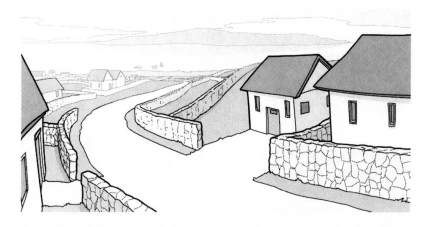

Aside from the mist and the random rock walls, there was not a soul in sight. It's a very strange feeling when there is not a soul in sight.

Incidentally, "not a soul in sight" means you don't see any people anywhere, even though you can see houses and buildings, and it seems like you should be able to see people.

There was a cluster of houses and small

buildings just up the hill from the ocean. We could see a church, too. It was the tallest building around. The center of town. It was the only place we could see that looked like humans might be there.

"Hurry, let's go!" I said.

We started to run up the hill. In a town that small, we were sure the first person we saw would know Séamus. Hau hovered clumsily after us yelling, "Wait up, mates!"

As we hurried toward the tiny town, we walked past a few dozen sheep, a handful of goats, and one very happy horse. Animals love Hau and he made sure to quickly pat each one as he flew by. He can understand animal language, which comes in very handy sometimes. Most people don't think animals are paying attention, but, believe me, they are.

"That horse told me he is happy 'cause he's

getting a carrot soon! Am I getting a carrot soon?" Hau wondered aloud.

We came to a house and saw a woman putting a sign on her door that said "Back in 5 minutes."

Ciarán and I ran up to her while Hau hid behind a rock wall. Those things sure do come in handy.

"Excuse me, Miss!" said Ciarán.

She jumped and dropped her purse.

"Ah me, ya nearly scared the pants off me!" she said.

> Incidentally, "scaring the pants off someone" just means you surprised them so much that they felt like their pants would fly right off. But they never actually do.

She told us it was usually so quiet on Inishmaan that we just surprised her by being there.

"What is it ye need?" she asked.

"We are looking for Séamus, do you know where he lives?" Ciarán said.

"Which Séamus? You know, we've got five here on the island," she said.

I turned to Ciarán and said, "I guess Séamus is a pretty popular name here?" He nodded his head. "Quite."

Ciarán said, "Do you know one that's got about 10 or 11 years?"

"Oh, yes, the young Séamus," she said. "Quite a troublemaker that one."

"That's the Séamus," I thought.

Then she added, "but he's good lad at heart, always helping folks round up their sheep when they jump the walls and whatnot, and quite a hurler he is."

Good lad? I doubted that.

"Do you know where we might find him?" Ciarán asked.

"Oddly enough, you just missed him. I saw him run past here only minutes ago, and in quite a rush, it seems. He was heading that way. He lives up there just past the pub, in a yellow house with blue trim," she said, pointing toward the church.

We said "thank you" in English, and in Irish "go raibh maith agat," and she rushed off in the opposite direction.

Just at that moment, Hau tumbled over to us

and landed in a heap at our feet, pebbles flying everywhere.

"Dude, are you OK?" I asked.

Hau was all out of breath and trying to tell us something. "Huuuffffdoooogggg, huuuuffftaaapppppee, hufffffgrrreeeeenn..."

Finally, he just held something up. In Hau's long fingered hand was another piece of the green tape from Ciarán's hurley. We were getting close!

11 FINN MCCOOL

We pulled out the other piece of tape we had found at the beach. It was a match!

"Where did you find this, Hau?"

"See that super duper friendly dog over there?" He pointed to this awesome looking black dog that was standing on a—you guessed it—rock wall.

We walked over to the dog, and he immediately put his paw on my shoulder, like we were old friends. Coolest dog ever.

"Well, I was hiding, like you tell me to do, and then he came up to lick

my face. His name is Finn McCool. Isn't dat COOL! McCool! Get it, Sey? He had dat tape in his mouth, too. He wanted to play war-of-tug with me. But den I memembered the hurley tape and I asked him nice if I could borrow it," explained Hau.

"Nice work, pal, the hurley must be really close!" We each gave Finn McCool and quick scratch on the head. Then, Ciarán grabbed Hau like a football. "I'll give you a lift, mate. Let's go!"

We raced past the church and up to the house next to the pub. There was only one yellow house with blue trim after the pub, so it was easy to find.

From the front gate we could see Séamus inside! That dirty rat! I could finally get a good look at him. He was a skinny kid with fluffy red hair and a very round face. He didn't actually look like a rat at all.

He was talking to his mother, and she didn't

look happy. She had her hands on her hips. We couldn't hear what she was saying, but I'm pretty sure she was using his first AND middle name.

"Mates, follow me," Ciarán said.

Ciarán started to open the gate. The gate was SUPER squeaky. A squeaky gate is the last thing you need when you're sneaking around.

I was holding the gate open for Hau when a gust of wind blew it out of my hand. SLAM!! Have

I mentioned the wind on Inishmaan? We all froze. I guess a SLAMMING squeaky gate is the last thing you need when you are sneaking around.

We looked up at the window, and Séamus was still talking to his mother. Luck of all lucks, they hadn't noticed us. Maybe it was the luck of the Irish?

We made our way around to the back of the house and LO AND BEHOLD, we found Séamus's backpack! Last time we saw that backpack, the hurley was in it while Séamus was riding off in his boat.

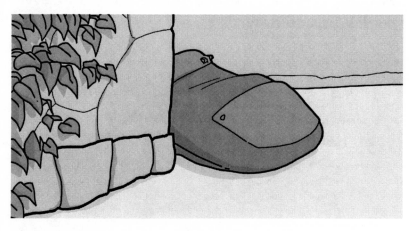

Incidentally, "lo and behold" is something you say when you find something you're surprised about.

The backpack was just lying there, ready for us to grab the hurley and get back to Spiddal for the big game!

"YES!!!" I thought. We still had 1 hour and 44 minutes. It wasn't much time, but it was enough.

Ciarán rushed over and opened it up, and Hau and me were right behind him.

"NOOOOOO!!" Ciarán said, as he fell to his knees.

Lo and behold, the bag was empty! Hau stuck his whole head in there to make sure, and even shook it upside-down.

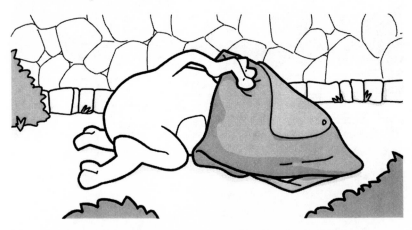

"Empty as my stomach feels, guys! Which is really empty. Got a burger lying around?" said Hau.

We just stood there staring at the empty backpack, not sure what to do next. We were flabbergasted.

Incidentally, "flabbergasted" is when you are so super surprised about something you can't even believe it.

When you mix "low and behold" with "flabbergasted" you are really in a bad situation.

We were in a bad situation.

12 SÉAMUS WILLIAM

We were just about to come up with a plan, when suddenly, Séamus walked out of the back door!

As shocked as we were to see him, he was even more shocked to see us. I think he was mostly shocked to see Hau. Obviously.

All 4 of us stood frozen in place. None of us could speak for what seemed like a million years,

but it was actually only about .42 seconds.

Finally, Hau broke the silence. "Sup, Dawg?" he said, as he slid on a pair of sunglasses that he pulled out of his pouch. He really watches too much TV. Anyway, it was enough to snap us all out of it.

"Where's my hurley, you, you, hurley stealer!" Ciarán yelled.

"Wha, wha, what is that?" stuttered Séamus, pointing at Hau.

"I'm your worst nightmare!" said Hau in his meanest voice, which really just sounds like a little old lady voice.

"Never you mind, Séamus! I know you took me hurley! Give it back, now!" Ciarán shouted.

He was all fired up! My soccer coach gets all fired up at the referee sometimes, and then they make him go sit in his car for the whole game.

Séamus didn't argue at all. He just bowed his head in shame and said, "I'm sorry. I don't know what I was tinking. I got a nasty cut on my finger and I didn't tink I would play well today. I tought if I took your hurley we'd surely win tonight. But when I got home, me mum knew something was about and she asked me what I had done. Ya can't lie to your mum, so I told her. She ain't too happy wit me right now. She called me Séamus William and told me I had to return the hurley immediately.

I was just comin outside to get it. She told me I'd find no joy in it if we won the big match, because I cheated. I'm ashamed. And I'm so, so sorry, mate. Do you forgive me?"

Welp, I wasn't expecting that. We're you?

I actually felt kind of bad for Séamus. He was right, cheating is no way to win. And you could tell he felt really horrible about it.

Hau, of course, was a big forgiver. He hugged Séamus and said, "Never do dat again, got it?"

"Got it," said Séamus, a bit surprised from being hugged by an alien and a bit slimy, 'cause, you know, Hau.

Ciarán wasn't as sympathetic. "Never mind how sorry you are, where is my hurley?" he blurted out.

Séamus, pointed to his backpack. "It's in there."

"We just looked in there! It's empty!" said Ciarán, super frustrated.

"What do you mean?" said Séamus, as he picked up the empty backpack. "WHAT?!? Oh, no! Where is it?"

"You tell us," Ciarán scowled. His voice told me that he did not forgive Séamus yet.

"I swear it was right in there. I was just coming out to get it and bring it back to you!" Séamus exclaimed. "I have an extra hurley. You can have it!"

"I need mine, or I can't play. That's the way it is," said Ciarán, very matter-of-fact.

"I understand, mate. I do," said Séamus.

Looked like we were back to the drawing board.

Incidentally, "back to the drawing board" is when you have to make a new plan because your first plan didn't work out so well.

I looked at Ciarán. "Don't worry, mate. We got this!" I told him in my most positive sure voice, even though I was not so positive sure.

1 hour 26 minutes. Things were not looking good.

13 SO MANY PRINTS

Séamus told us that he had left the bag outside so his mom wouldn't see it. We all started searching around the yard. Hau looked in a tree "for good measure," he told me.

We all found nothing. No hurley. No clues.

Ciarán looked like he was about to give up. He walked over to Séamus. I was slightly worried he was going to give him the ultimate "what for."

But something way different happened.

"You better go, mate. The game starts soon. No sense in both us missin' it," said Ciarán to Séamus.

Séamus put his hand on Ciarán's shoulder. "I'm not going unless you are. I got you into this mess, and I'm going to help get you out. Don't tell me you're giving up now! We've still got time, and I've

got a boat to get us back to Spiddal! We just need a little luck."

"Rectangle fingerprint, hurley boot-print, boat-print, dog paw print. So many prints today, huh Seymour?" said Hau. "I wish I would see a pizza print!"

"Haha! Yeah, you're right Hau. Lots of prints today. But no paw prints. You made a mistake," I told him.

"Yes, dere is! Right here! I think YOU are mistaken, sir!" said Hau as he pointed to some fresh paw prints.

We all stood around the paw prints. They led over the wall in Séamus's yard.

"Paw prints?! Of course! Finn McCool was in the yard when I got home. He's always wandering around everyone's yard. I hadn't remembered because my mum had me all freaked out. Do you think Finn took it?" Séamus said.

"Hey, we just met Finn McCool a few blocks away, and he had a piece of Ciarán's hurley tape! We just thought it had fallen off when you ran past him," I said. I turned to Hau. "Um, Hau?"

"Um, yes?" said Hau.

"Any chance Finn McCool mentioned the hurley?" said Seymour.

"No, he just told me he wanted to play war-of-tug wit da tape. And den he said he had to go play with his new giant bone."

Séamus looked perplexed. "Finn McCool can talk?"

Perplexed = completely baffled
(Completely baffled = confused or mixed up)

"Hau can talk to animals, now LET'S GO!!! Finn's "new giant bone" has got to be Ciarán's hurley!"

This was no hunch. I just knew it. Maybe we could still make it to the game. We all bolted out of the squeaky gate and raced back down the road,

past the pub, back to the "Back in Five Minutes" sign where we had last seen Finn McCool.

We hopped over the rock wall that Finn McCool was standing on. There was no time to ask permission.

"Finn McCool!!" we all called out. "Here, Finn McCool. Come, boy. We have treats!"

Hau said, "We do?!? Hook a pal up?"

Finn McCool was nowhere to be seen. What we did see, however, was an imprint of Ciarán's hurley in the wet ground.

Hau was right. So many prints!

As my grandpa would say, "Close, but no cigar." That means that we almost succeeded in our plan, but then we failed.

Incidentally, cigars are SO GROSS, and so is smoking. But I bet you already knew that. YUCK!"

79

We had to find that dog!! We had less than an hour until game time.

14 PUFFING HOLE

We hopped back over the wall ready to spread out and find Finn McCool, when we bumped right into the Back in Five Minutes lady, who was still not back at her store. Once again, she jumped and dropped her purse. Hau stuffed himself in the backpack before she saw him.

"AHHH! Oy! Not again, boys!" she said.

We were lucky again and her pants did not get scared off. We were extra lucky that she didn't see Hau, or I bet you can guess what would have happened.

Incidentally, it had been at least 30 minutes since she put the "Back in Five Minutes" sign on her door. I asked Ciarán about it and he said those things are not taken literally in Ireland.

"Hello lads, I see you found Séamus," she said, once she gathered her wits.

Incidentally, "wits" are like when you get yourself calmed down again after you got upset or surprised or can't stop laughing 'cause your friend Elliot told the best joke ever.

"Yes, tank you," said Ciarán. "Now we are looking for the dog that lives here. Have you seen him?"

"Finn McCool? I have," said the lady. "He was just heading toward the water with what looked like a big giant bone or stick or somethin'." She pointed down the road.

"Me hurley!!" Ciarán shouted as he dashed off. We scrambled off after him yelling, "Thanks so much! Bye!" I heard Hau yell from inside the backpack, "We will be back in five minutes!" and then he starting cracking up in there.

When we were out of sight, I let him out of the backpack and he hung on to the outside of it. I figured we needed all eyes on the lookout for Finn McCool.

We darted and dashed down the hill toward the water, occasionally jumping over a rogue sheep in our path. I had to run at my top speed to keep up with Séamus and Ciarán. They were faster than me, and I'm pretty fast. Guess you have to be super fast if you're the best hurler on your team.

Every once in a while we saw paw prints, but we still didn't see Finn McCool. The coast was super rocky, and the ocean sprayed big giant pillars of water up and over the rocks. It looked SO

AWESOME. Between the water and the wind it was really loud, and, aside from us, there was still not a soul in sight.

We were doing our best. Séamus was running back and forth looking over and around as many rock walls as he could. Ciarán was climbing on a wall trying to get a better view. I was scanning up and down the coast looking and we were all still yelling at the top of our lungs, "HERE, FINN MCCOOL!! COME ON, BOY! WE HAVE TREATS!!"

Suddenly, I realized that Hau wasn't with me. Had he blown off in the wind? I had a moment of panic until I heard him squealing with laughter. Phew!

I turned toward the sound and saw Hau high atop a water spout, thoroughly enjoying himself.

Séamus told us later that those spouts are called "puffing holes" and that you probably should stay away from them, unless you are a mega-galactic alien who can sort-of fly. He said people like to watch them from a distance and that they are awesome but dangerous. Duly noted.

Incidentally, "duly noted" means that you totally understand and you will be sure to remember that for next time.

The puffing hole shot Hau SUPER HIGH up into the air. So high, in fact, that he could see the entire island. Bingo! I had an idea... and Finn McCool was his name-o! Heh, heh, heh. Get it?

"HAU!" I yelled at the top of my lungs. He couldn't hear me over the crashing waves. I used our special call: "HAU NOW!!"

That did it. He looked over at me.

"Do you see Finn McCool from up there? Look around!!" I shouted.

He stood up and balanced on the water spout like a pro. He even got on his tip toes. He smiled, and his eyes got huge, like flying saucers, and he pointed up the hill to the old stone fort and said "GINN MCFOOL! BINN MCDROOL! FINN MCCOOL! I see him!!"

15 THE FORT

Man, that dog gets around. We hurled (Get it, "hurled"?) ourselves toward the old stone fort. It was all the way back at the top of the hill and the wind and the mist didn't make it easy to run. Still, we had to get there. We were almost out of time, and this was our last chance. We pressed on.

The old stone fort was called Dún Chonchúir, and it was BIZARRE! Dún Chonchúir is pretty hard to pronounce, but you can also call it Conor's Fort. We had to climb a little hill and spiral through this wild little rocky path to get in. Once we got inside, I realized it was a circle.

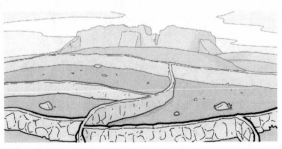

No one even knows how it got there or who made it, but it's very old and very awesome.

The moment we burst into the fort we saw him. There he was. Finn McCool. Sleeping soundly with Ciarán's hurley snuggled up under his paw.

As silently as possible, we ran toward Finn McCool. We didn't want him to wake up and run away. That would put us back at square one.

Incidentally, "back at square one" is when you have to start ALL OVER AGAIN. And we most definitely didn't have time for that!

When we reached Finn McCool he woke up, opened his eyes and started wagging his tail so fast you could barely see it. He got up, pounced over to Hau and started licking his face, leaving the hurley where it was.

Ciarán ran right over to the hurley, picked it up and did his own little happy dance with the hurley as his partner.

"Is it okay?" asked Séamus.

Ciarán inspected his hurley from handle to bas. (See, I'm learning the lingo.)

"Tá, it looks fine. There are a couple new teeth marks in it but nothing serious. Looks perfect to me," Ciarán said, smiling the biggest smile I had seen on him all day.

I could tell that "tá" meant "yes" in Irish.

Then Ciarán looked very seriously at Séamus. "I forgive you, mate."

"Thanks, mate. I'm so sorry, and I will never do that again," said Séamus. And I believed him.

"And, I hope you can forgive me," said Ciarán.

"For what?" asked Séamus.

"For beating you in the championship game today!" Ciarán laughed. "Now let's get to your

boat! We've got to get to the pitch!"

"Come on, Hau!" I called, holding my backpack open.

Hau let Finn McCool get in a final lick and he jumped into the backpack. "All this finding is making me starving," he said. I promised to get him a treat just as soon as I could. "Duly noted," he stated.

I looked at my watch. We only had 32 minutes to get back in time for the game. Could we even make it?

16 PETE'S SAKE

"I'll meet you at the dock!" yelled Séamus, as he raced home to grab his kit and his own hurley. He still had his hurley boots on from the morning. He told me later that on game day he wears his hurley boots all day. It's his personal tradition.

We got down to the dock in minutes with Hau jostling around in the backpack. "Now I think I AM Sey sick." He groaned. And then he giggled at his own joke.

Séamus was right on our heels with all of his gear in hand. Man, was he fast! He even handed Ciarán some new tape to rewrap his hurley.

"I always keep an extra bit around," Séamus smiled. "Thanks, mate," said Ciarán.

We jumped in the boat and Séamus started the motor and sped off into the ocean.

SPLASH, SLOSH, SPLASH, BOUNCE! It was a rough and fast ride. Hau climbed out of my backpack and onto my lap. I held on to him tight, like a beachball. A slimy, smelly beachball.

We were whizzing and zooming across the Atlantic Ocean toward Spiddal. We seemed to be making really good time! Soon I could see the beach where we would pull the boat up on the sand and run to the hurling pitch, when all of a sudden... the boat's motor quit working.

Putt, putt, putt, sputter, pop, plahhhhhhhPPT... and then nothing. Silence. We were flabbergasted.

"Oh, for Pete's sake!" cried Hau. It's possible Hau needs less screen time.

Incidentally, "oh, for Pete's sake" means "You have GOT to be kidding me!" I did not disagree.

We all looked at each other with worried faces. Séamus turned to the motor and started pulling the rope thing, trying to get the motor started. He pulled and pulled and pulled. Nothing.

We were so close we could actually hear the sound of the crowd at the pitch, ready for the championship hurling game. It was going to start any minute.

After all that work we were not going to get Ciarán and Séamus back in time for the big game.

I was out of plans and out of ideas and out of drawing boards. And, we were out of time.

I looked around to see if there was anyone who

could help, but there was no one out there.

Just then, a seagull landed on the edge of the boat. Hau went over and whispered something in his ear. At least I think it was his ear. Turns out, it was the same seagull that was tickling Hau when we arrived.

The seagull made a really loud SQUAWK and seconds later, two dolphins popped their heads up next to the boat.

"What are you dudes waiting for? Throw dem a rope!" Hau ordered.

Séamus looked confused but obeyed and tossed the dolphins a rope.

They made some cool dolphin sounds, grabbed the rope and started pulling us toward the beach!! They were even faster than the motor!! Dolphins RULE!! And the seagull, too. And Hau, of course. The magical, mysterious, awesomest pal ever, Hau! He always saves the day.

In no time flat, we were out of the boat and pulling it up on the sand.

Incidentally, "in no time flat" means when you get there faster than you even thought you could. My mom always says that to make me feel better when we are running late for my friend's birthday party.

I plopped Hau in the backpack, and we ran toward the pitch. Hau protested, "Aw, man! I want to watch."

"Don't worry, pal, I'll let you peek out." I told him.

We could see the teams were just starting to take the field.

3 minutes till game time!

17 THE BIG GAME

Séamus dashed to toward his locker room. "Good luck, mate! You'll need it," he smiled at Ciarán.

Ciarán laughed. "You'll be the one needin' the luck."

Ciarán had his hurley in hand but realized he didn't have the rest of his kit. He couldn't play in what he was wearing! He HAD to have his uniform on, and he needed his hurling boots, too!

Luck was on our side, AGAIN. We turned to see Róisín standing there holding up Ciarán's bag filled with his kit and his boots. Ciarán smiled from ear to ear, picked her up, gave her a spin in the air and said, "Best sister, ever." Then he grabbed his bag and ran into the locker room.

Róisín and me went to sit down in the stands to watch. I opened the backpack a little so Hau could see. Róisín had brought a bag full of fish and chips for Hau to eat, which almost made him leap for joy out of the backpack. "Best sister, ever," Hau repeated. She really was.

CHIPS =  CRISPS=

Incidentally, "Fish and Chips" in Ireland means a piece of fried fish and some french fries. Not fish with potato chips. In Ireland, chips = french fries. If you want potato chips you have to ask for "crisps." Potato chips = crisps. Might want to write that one down for future reference.

Moments later, Ciarán and Séamus came running onto the pitch, just as the whistle blew to start the game. The crowd cheered!

Wow! They made it! Phew!!

I was PSYCHED to watch the hurling match.

What a cool sport! You have got to go see a match sometime. The game went back and forth and back and forth. It's so fast. I can't believe I had never heard of such a great game. The players were running with the sliotar bouncing on their hurley, and picking it up off the ground and whacking it toward the goal. They never stopped running. I really wished I could jump in there and play, too. I was thinking that I might start a hurling team when I got back home.

Halfway through the game I looked around, and you won't even believe who I saw. Salty Dog! He was standing near the bleachers. Even though his arms were crossed and he looked kinda grumpy, I could see a little smile on his face.

I heard a kid behind me whisper and point, "Hey look, there's old Fred! All-Ireland hurling champion from back in the day. He was one of the best hurlers in the country. He was the Man of the

Match! Let's go get a photo with him."

He was pointing at Salty Dog. The medal he wore around his neck! It was an All-Ireland Championship medal. I only have one thing to say about that. Awesome.

At that moment he looked over at me and gave me a thumbs up. I smiled and did the thumbs up back.

Incidentally, "Man of the Match" means the best player. Like the MVP. Which means he's amazing at hurling.

The game was nearing the end. Both Ciarán and Séamus had gotten 4 points and 1 goal for their teams, which means they had each scored a total of 7 points so far. It was hard for me to know who to root for, 'cause now they were both my pals.

It was down to the last minute. The score was 14-12, and Séamus's team was winning. The referee was looking at his watch and had his

whistle in his mouth, about to blow to end the match.

Séamus had the sliotar and was about to pass it up field when one of Ciarán's teammates knocked it off his hurley and quickly passed it to Ciarán. He caught it, ran for three steps, balanced it on his hurley while running at top speed, popped it over the head of a defender and took a big swing, cracking it in the back of the net just as the referee blew his whistle. Three points!!! **Ciarán's team won 15 -14!**

The crowd went wild! Róisín went wild! I went wild! I zipped Hau inside the backpack so he could go wild and not fall out! It felt like my backpack was filled with a pack of squirrels having a dance party.

Ciarán ran all over the field like a swooping airplane as his whole team chased him and hoisted him up on their shoulders. Just like Charlie in my soccer game! He held his hurley high above his head like a trophy.

You could tell Séamus and his teammates were SUPER BUMMED out. But they lined up, and both teams walked past to shake hands.

"Good game." "Good game." "Good game." "Good game," the players said as they walked past one another.

I could hear Hau inside the backpack. "Good game. Good game. Good game. Good game," he said. He cracks me up.

Séamus and Ciarán were last in line. They stood facing each other.

"Good game, mate," said Ciarán to Séamus. "Close one, aye."

"One of these days, you know, we will play in the All-Ireland match for County Galway, and we'll be teammates." said Séamus.

You see, with hurling, even though they play against each other when they're kids, they will play on the same team when they grow up, since they both live in County Galway.

"Unstoppable teammates," said Ciarán.

Then he put his arm over Séamus's shoulder, and they walked back to the locker room together.

18 MATES

It was time for us to take The Leap home. Somehow, we had found the hurley and gotten Ciarán to his game in time. It was another great adventure, and I couldn't wait to come back to Ireland someday. Hopefully soon.

The sun was starting to set, and the sky looked absolutely incredible. It was pinks and blues and oranges over the Atlantic Ocean. It was really clear, and I could see Inishmaan out in the distance. The middle island.

The field was empty, and everyone had gone home. Róisín was playing with Hau. She was teaching him how to hold the hurley and how to pick up the sliotar and smack it with the bas end of the hurley. He tried and tried and kept missing the sliotar and spinning around like a top. Then

he would laugh and say, "Swing-and-a-miss!" and Róisín would crack up.

I found out later that Róisín was the best player on her team, too! She plays camogie, which is basically the exact same thing as hurling, only the team is all girls. It's just as awesome and fast and rough as hurling.

Ciarán and Séamus came out of the locker room. Without any warning they both hoisted me up on their shoulders and ran me around the field. Róisín

put Hau on her shoulders and ran him around, too.

"Three cheers for Seymour and Hau!!" they all yelled. "Hip, hip hooray!! Hip, hip hooray!! Hip, hip hooray!!"

They set us down. Hau gave Róisín a huge squashy hug, and then proceeded to hug Ciarán and Séamus.

"Go raibh maith agat. Thank you, Seymour. You'll always have a cara here in Ireland," said Ciarán, using the Irish word for friend. We shook hands.

"Two chairde," smiled Róisín.

"Tree cairde," said Séamus. And he pulled his extra hurley and a sliotar out of his bag and gave it to me. "Go on and practice now so when ye come back again we can play." Séamus was SO COOL, after all.

Now I had my own hurley and sliotar! NO WAY!

Hau pouted until I promised him I would share.

"And you will always have a mate in the United States," I told them.

"And don't forget, pals, there's always room for a Full Irish!" said Hau.

They all stood waving as we walked away, calling out "slán abhaile" which means, "safe trip home".

Hau pulled out the TELLUS and pushed the "LEAP HOME" button.

The leap home is exactly the same as the leap that takes us all around the world EXCEPT... backwards. Like this:

1. You swing upside-down
2. Shoot left
3. Shoot right
4. Go down, then up (like a wave)
5. Slinky spin
6. Stomach falls down to your toes
7. Drop down a hill
8. Fly up a hill
9. Hear a loud RUMBLE (that's really Hau's stomach)
10. Step out of the closet and into my bedroom

It is SO FUN! You HAVE to try it sometime.

19 HOME

We appeared in my closet at the exact same time we left home. Back the same day we left, as my grampa would say.

The TELLUS is really SO AMAZING. I wish I knew how it works, but I don't. I tried to ask Hau once, and he just said in a deep funny voice, "When you're ready, my child," followed by, "Got any fruit snacks?"

Ireland was amazing. Ciarán and Róisín were telling me about all of the other cool places to go, for when I come back. I want to check out The Cliffs of Moher, which are these magical beautiful cliffs not too far away from Spiddal. They told me about this place called The Burren, which is this mysterious rocky land that looks like you landed on a planet in a galaxy, far, far away. There are tons of castles to explore, cities, waterfalls, and cool stuff no matter which direction you go! Plus, I still need to see Inishmore and Inisheer. There's also an awesome old hurley making place in Kilkenny that has been making hurleys for over 50 years!

THE CLIFFS OF MOHER

CASTLES

THE BURREN

DUBLIN

I grabbed my favorite book, Guinness World Records™. I was curious if there was anything about hurling in there. I found out about the biggest hurling match ever, with 916 hurlers playing in the match, and the longest hurling match ever, which lasted for 24 hours 14 minutes and 2 seconds. Whoa!! That is WILD! Both of these winning records took place in Ireland, of course! The county of Kilkenny, where Ciarán's mom is from, has had the most All-Ireland championship wins ever so far.

Incidentally, Guinness World Records™ actually STARTED in Ireland. Can you believe that? It was started to settle a bet between friends and just got super popular from there. It is SO AWESOME.

I could hear Hau snoring in the closet. Adventure really makes him sleepy. He was talking in his sleep, as usual. "Fish, chips, mates, sliotars, Full Irish, hurley, Finn McCool, more Full Irish..."

Before I hopped into bed, I had to do my personal tradition. I found Ireland on my map and pressed a thumbtack into the west coast of

Ireland, almost in the middle of the shoreline. County Galway, Ireland. Check.

I don't like to go to bed, but sometimes I will rest my eyes. This time when I rested my eyes, I fell asleep in 4.2 seconds. Isn't that bizarre?

Slán! Goodbye!

THE END

Melanie Morse and Thomas McDade currently live Buffalo, NY where it's actually pretty great. You should all come and check it out. When they aren't walking their super cute dog, Honey, or traveling with some particularly fun kids (also quite cute) they can be found producing and directing video projects and commercials with their company Honey + Punch.

seymourandhau.com
honeyandpunch.com